HEMINGWAY'S CHIHUAHUA

AND OTHER MYSTERIES

Direction artistique : Jamie Keenan
Mise en page : JOUVE

Enregistrements, montage et mixage : Studio Corby
Texte lu par Saul Jephcott et Karin Morgan

© Les Éditions Didier, Paris, 2011 - ISBN 978-2-278-06952-1 - Imprimé en France
Dépôt légal : 6952/02
Achevé d'imprimer par EMD S.A.S. en mars 2012 - N° 26306

Hemingway's Chihuahua

AND OTHER MYSTERIES

Peter Flynn

didier

Some of these stories happened, and some of them did not.

Did Hemingway own an invincible Chihuahua? Does The Queen play poker? Did Einstein teach his chauffeur the secrets of Relativity? Did Josephine Baker's beast attack an orchestra in Paris?

Which of these stories are true, and which ones are false?

It's for you to decide...

True or False?

Check your answers on www.paperplanes.fr

Einstein's
Chauffeur

THE PODIUM HIDES HALF MY BODY but it can't
conceal my trembling hands. I take a deep breath,
place his glasses on my nose, and look down at his
notes. They are in German. I can't read German.
Why? Because I'm from Pittsburg. I shouldn't even
be up here.

I look around the amphitheatre full of
researchers: there are grey heads, white heads,
bald heads and young heads with alert, enthusiastic expressions. A hall full of physicists who want
to learn from me. I'm a chauffeur, and I'm here to
teach Relativity.

I clear my throat and take a drink of water.
At the back of the amphitheatre I see a familiar

figure dressed in my dark chauffeur's uniform, sitting on a stool with my cap pulled down over his eyes. Even from here I can see his white hair. He sits up and I see the quick, childish smile come across his face. He sticks his tongue out at me.

Now the crowd is becoming agitated. There is a noise of chairs moving, and I'm thinking they can smell my fear, they've got to know what's up. But now my boss is smiling and I can feel his warmth right from the back of the hall.

I can't blame him. He didn't force me to do this. I gave him the idea and he just...persuaded me. I've been driving him for a couple of months now, and one thing I can tell you for certain, it's hard to say no to the professor. Just last week, as I was driving Professor Einstein back from a conference in Baltimore, I remember his calm Austrian accent coming from the back of the car.

"Harry, did you enjoy the speech I made this evening?"

"Oh, absolutely, sir."

"Yes...I saw that you were enjoying it. I had a very good view."

"Sir?"

"It appears to me that you were in a state of repose at the back of the auditorium. Is that correct?"

I slowed down a little, and glanced up at him in the mirror.

"Repose? What do you mean, sir?"

"You were asleep, yes. That is correct, is it not?"

I took a second to think about that. There wasn't any anger in his voice, just curiosity. I guess you'd call it a desire for knowledge. His dark eyes were watching me in the mirror.

"Well, I wouldn't say I was asleep—"

"Harry, we have, how do you put it...we have been on the road for some months now, yes? And although for many people across America my theory is new, you have heard me explain it at least twenty times, is that correct?"

"Twenty-three times, sir."

He chuckled and slapped his knees. "Exactly. I can see it clearly. Now, you cannot read a book twenty-three times and expect to stay interested, can you?"

"No sir, I imagine that would be difficult."

He sat back for a few minutes and I drove on through the rain. It was an easy drive back to the hotel, but I was going slowly as I thought he had something more to say.

"Harry," he said at last. "Am I boring?"

"Oh no, sir."

"But my speech is boring you, yes?"

"Oh no, Mr Einstein. I wouldn't say that at all. I guess I've just heard the old Theory of Relativity so many times, I could give your speech myself."

"Really?"

For a moment I thought I'd gone too far. He sounded angry.

"Please, prove it," he said.

"Well, sir..." I began. And I gave him his introduction, word for word. He sat back in the seat, laughing softly.

"I don't mean to be disrespectful, sir, it's just that I have a good memory—"

"An *excellent* memory," he said. "And what about the central theme, hmm?"

I gave him the rest of the speech, without having any idea what it all meant. I even did it with an Austrian accent, as I'd spent a long time sitting at the back of conference halls mouthing out the words as he said them.

"Fascinating," he said when I'd finished. "I couldn't have put it any better! I can't blame you for falling asleep. I've often felt a little drowsy myself, saying the same thing each time."

"But it's important, Mr Einstein! I'm sure lots of people hang on to your every word!"

"Yes…"

"One day it could even make you famous."

He sat back in the seat so I couldn't see him, and we drove on for another few minutes. Then he bounced forward, wringing his hands in his lap, his eyes wide and childish.

"Stop the car."

I pulled over to the side of the road, and we sat for a few minutes. I remember the sound of the rain on the roof, like a hundred ticking clocks, and the shape of the physicist in the back of the cab, thinking.

"I think we can have a little fun, yes? Some refreshment. We go to Dartmouth next week… no one there knows me, not yet…no one knows what I look like. So, why not you go and give the speech, and I take a little repose at the back, yes?" He pulled at his bow tie and smiled in the dark.

I should have said no. Straight away I should have slammed the door on the idea, but Professor Einstein is one of those people it's very difficult to refuse. More than that, he's the kind of man who'll make you believe you can do anything. Anything I found difficult he'd just laugh away.

Over the next three days Professor Einstein spent a great deal of time explaining Relativity to me in simple terms a child might understand. He drew me pictures of a lift in a skyscraper, then one of trains pulling away from one another, and while I was no closer to understanding what the theory meant, his drive and his confidence were enough to make me agree to exchange clothes before we left the Dartmouth hotel, and he even persuaded me to let him drive us through the grounds of the university to the Physics Department.

So here I am at the front of this great hall, staring at the sheet of paper. I'm trying to remember what he told me in the hotel, but all I can see are trains and skyscrapers spinning away into a black hole. The other thing I can see is me getting discovered and handing my uniform to my boss for the last time. Einstein's tweed jacket is tight around my shoulders, and only now am I aware of how much smaller he is than me.

The faces at the front are all enthusiastic and attentive; I see one young man, sharp-eyed like a fox, his pen poised over his paper. I take a final look at my chauffeur at the back of the hall. He's already slumped in repose, his white hair frothing out from under his cap.

I begin.

I move through the speech, speaking slowly and carefully, not understanding a word I'm saying, but pretty soon I'm delivering the whole kaboodle word for word, just as we'd rehearsed it in the hotel. Just as the professor had told me, over and over again, "Don't think, Harry, don't think about it all. Just let the words come out in the right order." At first I'm numb, beyond thinking, but pretty soon I'm forgetting myself and just giving a good performance. Before I know it I'm finishing and feeling very clever and flushed with success as I gather up Einstein's notes.

Before anyone can stick up a hand to ask a question I'm rushing down off the stage, the professor's papers clasped to my chest, the hall ringing with the sound of applause.

I could do this all week, I'm thinking. *The hell with it. Let Einstein drive.*

I see him stand up at the back, clapping delightedly, smiling like the proudest uncle in the world. As if in a dream I go towards him—

—and the fox-faced student steps in front of me, speaking breathlessly.

"Excuse me, Professor. I very much enjoyed your talk."

"Why, thank you," I murmur, trying to push past.

"Perhaps if you could just elucidate on one point..."

The clapping is dying down and soon the other professors and researchers can hear what's being said. The Professor is now standing beside me but saying nothing. My knees are starting to tremble again, I feel the cold rise up in my guts once more.

"Elucidate," I mumble. *What does **that** mean?*

I look over at Albert Einstein for help, but he

just carries on looking proudly at me and not saying a word.

"Yes, sir," the student goes on. "You see, you argued that the principle proposed by Newton…"

I lose him from there on in. I have no idea what to say, I can only let him finish and wait for him to find me out. I wish Professor Einstein would come out and rescue me, but he just takes out the car keys and says, in a terrible Pittsburg accent, "Shall I wait outside, sir?"

The student is waiting, his pencil is poised on his pad. I notice four other students waiting in the same way, their pens quivering like stings. Over their shoulders I see Einstein stick out his tongue again, and suddenly it feels like his voice is speaking through me, his words slow and patient and logical.

I look straight at the student and put on my best Austrian accent.

"The answer to that is very simple," I say cheerfully. "Why, it's so simple, I'm going to let my chauffeur answer it!"

The Mystery

Albert Einstein (1879-1955) was born in the German Kingdom of Württemberg to a family of non-practising Jews. By the age of 10 he was reading Kant's philosophical works as well as important mathematical texts. In 1921, he was awarded the Nobel Prize in Physics.

It was Einstein who, during World War 2, convinced President Roosevelt that it was technically possible to build an atomic bomb and that the Germans might attempt to do so. As a result of his intervention, the Americans began the Manhattan Project, which culminated in the creation of the first atomic bomb and the destruction of Nagasaki and Hiroshima. Einstein, a pacifist and a particular lover of Japanese culture, was always troubled by his role in this.

During his career, Einstein travelled extensively around America and the rest of the world, lecturing on physics. He visited numerous American universities to talk about the theory of relativity *but...*

Did Albert Einstein really persuade his chauffeur to deliver a speech on Relativity?

Notes From
The Maestro

MY ONLY DISAPPOINTMENT is that I never saw him
until 1791. That was the year he died, and the year
he saved me from starvation. I was forty-two and it
had been many days since a warm meal had touched
my lips. That February I drank the snow from the
steps of the Vienna Opera House and dreamed of
hot soup and meat. My only real nutrition came
not from food or water, but music.

Music! I used to sit on the golden steps of the
opera house and wait for the great doors at the top
to open, breathing in the beautiful sounds that came
from within. Ah, the excitement of a clarinet con-
certo, released by a Philistine leaving the concert hall
early, or the aroma of a cantata coming from a bro-

ken window— it was so hard to resist throwing a stone when there was so much happiness to be heard and tasted. It was all that was keeping me alive.

Of course I knew I could never go in. Although I speak well, I have lived in this cape for fourteen years, my shoes are clinging to my feet and I smell of a decade of unwashed clothes. All I can do is sit on these steps and hope for charity from those lucky angels who can enter the hall, who can bathe in the serenades I can only taste, drop by drop, here in the heart of the Austrian winter.

His music, of course, was sent to him by God. Since I first heard news of him as a boy, touring Europe with his father, angering the Vatican with his perfect recollection of their liturgies, I was interested in him. But only when I heard his early compositions, when I was a student myself in happier times, did I feel happy in a way I couldn't explain. I could listen to his arrangements and endure all evil. As my position declined from a moderate family income to penury the composer grew more powerful, playing to emperors and audiences in Prague and England, and his name became famous everywhere.

That didn't mean anything to me until I sat outside on a night full of cold stars and sipped the notes I could hear coming from the broken window, or the rarely opened door. And even before that night in 1791 I was following his life through stories I heard in street markets; some too extraordinary to be true, such as his proposal of marriage to a young Marie Antoinette when he was a child. Or of the time he visited a farm when he was two years old, and when a pig squealed he cried "G-Sharp!" and the family ran to the nearest piano and found it to be true: a pig in G-Sharp.

Like me, he has experienced prosperity, and I know he has tasted poverty, too. I know of that winter, not long ago, when his commissions stopped, denying him the luxurious life he had become accustomed to. I heard that on some freezing evenings he would dance a waltz with his wife, just to keep warm.

That picture of him dancing with Constance came into my mind whenever I saw him hurrying to and from rehearsals at the Hall of Mirrors at Schloss Schönnbrunn. I was so sure it was him, a little man hunched up in thin clothes against the cold, but I never had the courage to act on my assumption, not until that night in February and I heard *Die Zauberflote*. I was enraptured, I was filled with the joy of his notes, and when the little figure came scurrying out of the great golden doors, I stepped in front of him. I was starving, you see.

"Please, Herr Mozart," I began, holding out a trembling hand. The woolen glove was frayed and wet from cupping snow to drink.

The composer had looked flushed with success when he'd emerged, but now he seemed anxious. He wore a purple pelisse and a cocked hat laced with gold, but he seemed sick, haunted even.

"What do you want?" His voice was soft, a tenor.

"Just some money for some bread," I said automatically, and felt humiliated by the words even as they came out. I bit my tongue.

"I wish I had some money," the composer said quietly. He kept his head lowered, a very thin, very pale man, with a puff of blonde hair and the vestiges of variola showing on his pitted face.

"Please, I know you've been poor," I said desperately. "I know you danced with Frau Constance just to keep her warm on penniless evenings, and your music has warmed me, it has warmed my very soul in the winter snow, Herr Mozart. I've danced with your music. It's told me so much about grace and loveliness, I pray you might have just a penny for me."

At the mention of his wife Mozart looked up and his eyes were extraordinary. I've seen huskies in Vienna with eyes like blue fire, and Herr Mozart's eyes were just such a colour. He looked straight through me; at the same time, his eyes were tinted with amusement, bright and alive.

From a pouch he produced a sheet of paper, a tiny inkpot and a quill. Opening the inkpot, he pushed it into my hand, dipped the quill and began writing. There was something powerful and energetic about the way he wrote, something joyful and frenzied at the same time. Within minutes I saw a composition appear, black on yellow paper, like crows in a field of corn.

When he'd finished he wrote a short letter, sealed it and gave me the sheet of music.

"A minuet and a trio," he said darkly. "Tomorrow morning you shall take it to the address on the envelope."

"But, I don't know...how..."

He gave a great childish smile at my confusion and walked off into the night. I stood for a few minutes, shivering under the stars, the precious paper hot in my hands. The notes were elegant and black, at once alien and imprints of the Divine. *Notes from the master*, I thought. *Real music, original music, music composed for me!*

I held onto it all night. I slept with the composer's ink still drying between my fingers, yet hunger drove me to the address of the publisher where, after much explanation, I exchanged Mozart's composition for five guineas.

That was the day that music brought me bread and meat and fine wine. I never saw Herr Mozart again, but now, whenever I hear one of his minuets, I remember his eyes the colour of fire, his ink on the golden page, his impulsive smile and the banquet he composed for me.

The Mystery

Wolfgang Amadeus Mozart (1756-1791) is among the most enduringly popular of all classical composers. A childhood prodigy, he began composing music at the age of five. The next years of his life were spent touring Europe with his father and sister, also musicians, performing for royalty wherever they went.

As an adult, Mozart settled in Vienna, where his lifestyle was considerably more expensive than his income permitted. He was soon in deep financial trouble and this would remain a cause of constant anxiety, despite the success of operas such as *The Marriage of Figaro* and *Don Giovanni*.

In September of 1791, Mozart fell ill and died two months later. He was just 35 years old when he died, and in the course of his short life had composed over 600 works of music ranging from opera to symphonies and concertos, chamber, piano and choral music, *but...*

Did Mozart ever write a short piece of music for a beggar?

Strangers in a Bar

IT WAS ABOUT ELEVEN O'CLOCK AT NIGHT, and it had either been raining or was just about to rain. Raymond Chandler was wearing his grey suit, with white shirt, striped tie and striped handkerchief, brown shoes and blue socks with pistols on them. He was everything an ambitious crime writer ought to be. He was writing a screenplay for Hitchcock.

The door of the Block Bar was made of green glass, with a faded sign saying OPEN FOR AUTHORS ONLY. One thing was obvious. Whoever came in here to write wasn't bothered by the creaking chairs or the faded tabletops or the dusty air.

Chandler frowned at the manuscript, imagining shadows in the rain. He couldn't hear the characters speaking in his mind. Goddamnit, why couldn't Hitchock employ him to write a script based on one of his *own* books?

He was just starting to enjoy the misery when a good-looking dame came in, shook out a black umbrella, and ordered a brandy straight up. *Journalist*, thought Chandler.

Arthur the barman served her a couple of shots and moved away.

She sat on a barstool, took a notebook from her coat and started writing in it. Her face lacked colour and it looked like she thought too much. After a while she sat back and quietly analysed Chandler.

"Blocked, aren't you?" she said.

"I can afford to be."

She put down her pen, mildly amused.

"How can you afford to be blocked?" she asked.

"For $2500 a week for five weeks, I can afford anything. Hollywood isn't cheap."

She raised an eyebrow and went back to her

note-taking. Chandler turned a page but nothing interested him. There was a long silence and Chandler felt uncomfortable, wondering why she wasn't asking him any questions.

Narrowing his eyes, he leaned over to the girl.

"Seeing as you're scratching away at that pad, I'd say *you're* the one who's blocked."

"I'm waiting for someone." A veil of brown hair fell across her right eye, making the other one bright and exquisitely mysterious. "It's what people do in bars."

"Don't get me wrong," Chandler went on. "Every chump gets blocked now and then. You know the score: we come here to loosen up a little, get flowing again."

He lit a cigarette without offering her one.

"The barman didn't even say hello to you," he went on. "I know him. He'd have to be ill not to try a move on a woman like you. Maybe he knows something I don't. I'd say you been down here before."

The woman clapped with soft hands. "Perceptive. And I bet you know it, too." He just puffed smoke and smiled. After a moment she took his arm and helped herself to his cigarette. Then she threw back her head as if she were laughing, and blew smoke out through her nose.

"*You* look more like the one who's waiting for inspiration."

"Not easy creating a screenplay from 250 pages of mush."

"One of your novels?"

He held up his hands and looked like a man denying all responsibility.

"*Strangers on a Train.*"

She slipped a silver cigarette case from her coat. Without offering one to Chandler she produced a lighter and sat back in a torrent of white smoke.

"So what's wrong with *Strangers on a Train*?"

"Writer's a friend of yours?" said Chandler.

"Let's say she is. Let's say I'm a fan. What's your problem with it?"

He coughed into his hand.

"The book. It's illogical."

"Oh?"

"Picture the scene," he said. "A perfectly nice young man agrees to murder a man he doesn't know in order to keep a maniac from tormenting him."

He coughed again. "Still, I'm aware that Ms Highsmith's still in her twenties, so this isn't a bad first effort. Just a little unrealistic."

"It's not unrealistic if you have the imagination."

"Well, there's the problem."

He heard her red nails drumming on the cigarette case, the squeak of her handbag.

"So you find the characters in the book implausible?" she said. "Difficult to bring to life in a movie?"

"Is this an interview?"

"Maybe."

He shook his head and mimed locking his lips with a key.

"You're just a big tease," she laughed. "You've no idea of how implausible characters can become. Take this one—" She slid a slim black book from an attaché case. "*The Big Sleep*. Have you read it?"

Chandler's jaw dropped slightly.

"You could say that."

"This has all you need to know about creating illogical characters. Take the women, for example…"

She flipped open the book.

"It's elegantly written, but how can we empathise with a lead character who's so obviously misogynistic? He's a beast."

Chandler watched her for a moment. His heart was beating a little faster than it should have been.

"We can't all be bright and clever and happy," he said.

She trailed a fingernail across the cover of his book. "Chandler's women *hiss*. They drool, they manipulate. Carmen's described as an animal."

Chandler smiled like a wolf waking from a nice sleep.

"She's just a young girl who wants Marlowe to pay attention to her."

"Garbage! She's a vehicle of hate—a tool of the author's chauvinistic desire. How can someone enjoy being called "Cute as a Filipino on Saturday night"?

Chandler shrugged and ordered a shot of whiskey. *You're pretty cute yourself*, he thought.

"At least he's a gentleman," he said. "Okay, he slaps her around a little, but it's pride that keeps him from sleeping with her, professional pride.

Picture the man: a bachelor comes home to his apartment and finds a beautiful naked girl in his bed. Sure, he's insulting, but he remains honourable."

"That's just a front." She glared at him. "He finds her repellent."

There was a note of triumph in her voice.

"He's a complex character," he said. "Not a *person*, but a *character*."

She snorted. "He seems impotent."

There was a silence. The dark-haired woman stared outside into the rain. A storm was building. Chandler found himself admiring the curve of her neck, her dark eyes, her arrogance. Once this was all over it might be a good idea rescuing this woman with a few extra-marital whiskies in a bar somewhere warm and secret.

He forced himself back to the screenplay. Nobody could help him with that. Hitchcock would dump him for another writer if he couldn't turn *Strangers on a Train* into a taut, believable script.

Quietly the young woman asked, "How about Agnes?"

"Huh?"

"Agnes in *The Big Sleep*. The blonde book-seller. Another malignant woman."

"Now you're being cruel. She's a swell lady."

"Not according to Marlowe. He tells her she looks like a Pekinese right after he's hit her with the butt of his gun."

He beamed. "He's as vicious towards women as he is to men. Now you're making it sound like all the girls in the novel are idiots or prostitutes."

She took a savage drag on her cigarette.

"And hideously exaggerated. How can a man as dour and emotionally retentive as Marlowe inspire not one, but two beautiful sisters to fall into his arms?"

Chandler sat back on his stool. She smelled extremely nice.

The woman checked her watch and scowled and returned to the attack. "Do you realise how difficult it is to empathise with a character with such ridiculous values? Or is Marlowe simply a tease?" Her eyebrow went up like a cat's tail.

"He's a professional," he said. "He's a para-doxical man who has his emotional moments."

"Yeah? And when do those happen?"

"Let's get this straight. He's not in this game to be a nice guy, he's not here to seduce women, he's here to gather information for his client. That's what makes him believable; not the work of a debutant."

There was a clap of thunder from outside. She looked away and Chandler finished his drink, convinced he had her beat. He had to admire her spirit. She was starting to grow on him.

He was just about to suggest they move someplace else when the door banged open and a gust of wind blew a small woman into the bar. She was holding a dilapidated umbrella in one hand, a fur hat in the other. Her face was flushed red by the freezing wind, and her heels clattered on the parquet floor. As she tottered forward in the feeble light, trying to smooth her chaotic hair, she looked back at the door and muttered,

"What fresh hell was *that*?"

Chandler's companion slid off her stool and bounced up to her.

"Dorothy! What took you so long?"

The new arrival gave a tired shrug.

"You know how it is. Always walking into the wind."

Smiling, the other woman took her hand and kissed it.

"I've been waiting for you," she said gently.

"Patty, let's get out of here. Get a real drink."

"Patty?" repeated Chandler.

"Ms Highsmith, to you," said the author, primly. "And that's my first novel you have there."

Chandler turned a soft tint of scarlet. His cigarette started to droop like an embarrassed flower. Patricia gave Chandler a hard smile and refused his outstretched hand.

"I already know who *you* are."

Dorothy Parker checked her make up in a razor-shaped mirror, lifted an expensive overcoat from a nearby stool and draped it over the other woman's shoulders. As they walked out of the bar, arm in arm, Patricia Highsmith called over her shoulder.

"You're Marlowe."

The door clanged shut. Chandler let the words sink in. Twenty seconds pounded by in his brain. Then he ordered a Scotch from the barman who'd seen everything. He could feel a hangover coming on, but this wasn't a hangover from alcohol.

It was from women.

"Women," he murmured. "Women make me sick."

The Mystery

Raymond Chandler (1888-1959) was an American novelist and pioneer of the modern detective story. He is famous as the inventor of Philip Marlowe, the archetypal tough, macho private detective. His Marlowe novels have been adapted numerous times for the cinema.

Patricia Highsmith (1921-1995) was an American novelist notable for her psychological thrillers and short stories, some two dozen of which have been adapted for the cinema, including her first novel, *Strangers on a Train*.

Dorothy Parker (1893-1967) was a writer and founder member of New York's Algonquin Round Table, famous for her quick wit. Her career was stopped when she was blacklisted because of her socialist political views.

All three of these writers were living and working in Los Angeles in the early 1940s, *but...*

Did Raymond Chandler unwittingly insult Patricia Highsmith in a Hollywood bar?

Josephine's
Beast

TOWARDS THE END OF 1927 a young American was lost backstage at the Folies Bergères. She held on to her violin case as she fought her way around fake palm trees and elephant foot stools, desperate to find the entrance to the orchestra pit. Her wing collar was sticky with sweat, and a strand of black hair kept escaping the cream she'd plastered on, only an hour ago.

Everyone was moving against her. Emily passed some African dancers, sitting around in loincloths, and asked them breathlessly how to find the orchestra pit, but none of them seemed to understand her French. Several chorus dancers rushed past, leaving memories of perfume and cigarettes, but none of them stopped for her. From somewhere nearby she heard the orchestra waking up. Now Emily started to panic, realising the show was about to begin and there'd be a gap in the string section where she ought to be.

"Josephine! Last call for Josephine! Where is she?" A fierce woman in a long grey skirt was standing beside a distortion mirror, frowning at a clipboard and giving orders to a terrified French boy.

"Excuse me, Madame…" began Emily.

"What?"

The woman turned and her reflection loomed up behind her. Her glasses gleamed like freshly polished pistols.

"My name is Emily Miller, I'm the replacement for—"

"Last call!" she screamed at the French boy. "Go get Josephine! We're all waiting for her! Where is she?"

"Would that be Miss Baker?" Emily asked politely.

"How perspicacious of you," snapped the steel-haired French woman. "How perceptive! What are you doing here? Get to your position!"

"Can you—"

"Positions!"

She disappeared behind the mirror, her heels clicking like ice picks. Everyone was running and shouting and laughing. The backstage nerves made Emily's heart beat even faster, wishing they'd given her more than an hour to get ready and cross the city for the show. She was a late stand-in: damn it, she hadn't even rehearsed with these guys, and now she was playing in the orchestra for the hottest show in town, the great Josephine Baker in her banana skirt.

Emily was too poor to buy a ticket to the show, but many of her friends had. How she dreamed of seeing Josephine Baker in person. Ask any young man about her and he'd roll his eyes and a big happy smile would cross his face and he'd tell stories about a wild woman dancing on stage, dark and lovely and naked. Hemingway had already called her "the most amazing woman anyone ever saw".

"Josephine! Where is she?" shrieked the French woman. "The audience is hungry!"

Emily ran around in circles, desperate for a stage door. Dwarves and dancers and white hunters pushed past her, and when she dropped her violin she had to search the floor for it in the dark.

Soon she found the case, but she couldn't pick it up. There was a svelte brown foot resting on top of it. Emily's eyes followed the foot up a long leg, up past a pair of white shorts, a half open blouse, a necklace of pearls and a round face, smiling in the obscurity.

"I need a hand," said the face.

It was a soft voice, French words perfumed with an American lilt. There was no hurry in that voice, no anxiety. Emily tried to say something but she was so shocked she couldn't find the words. The woman picked up her violin with one hand and took her by the elbow with the other.

"Naughty Francine is in a cupboard with one of the stage boys," said the dark woman. "Now I have no one to help me with my make up, but I'm sure you'll do."

Her hand found Emily's, her fingers smooth in her palm, and she pulled her down a narrow corridor. She moved in a grand, aggressive manner, her body muscular and graceful in the half-darkness. Somewhere in Emily's panicking mind she knew who she was. The woman led her through a squeaky door and into a purple dressing room. In one corner was a mirror surrounded by white lights, with various slips, a brassière and a bunch of bananas draped over the top of it. A black curtain covered the far side of the room. There was the smell of perfume and skin creams, mixed with something else, a musty, animal odour.

"Uh, Miss Baker, I'm looking for—"

Josephine Baker turned away and lifted off her blouse. Emily looked away. She felt as though she'd just swallowed a locomotive.

"You're an American," said Josephine, smiling over her shoulder.

"That's right, ma'am," croaked Emily. "I'm a violinist."

"A lady fiddler! Can't be many of you around." She touched Emily's hair. "Hey, I love the *bob*... where you from, Mississippi?"

"Savannah, Georgia."

"Honey, you see that bra hanging over the mirror? The white one? That's it. I need you to get that for me, now." She laughed. "That's all right, come a little closer, I don't bite—"

As she said this a growl came from behind the black curtain. Josephine clapped her hands and called out, "Chiquita!"

Another growl.

"Chiquita, you behave yourself, honey." Josephine turned to Emily. "You come round here by the stool and she can't reach you none. I need you to clip me up, that's all."

Swallowing, Emily approached so she was standing straight behind the long, smooth back. More than anything else in the world she wanted to reach out and run her fingers down her beautiful skin.

Josephine laughed. "We don't got all day, y'know."

With trembling hands, Emily reached round her with the bra, and the top of her hand brushed the smoothness of her breast. Josephine didn't react— but the animal behind the curtain growled again. Emily fumbled. The bra dropped. Both women bent down at the same time and Josephine's derrière bumped her cheek. They laughed, Josephine merrily, Emily a little nervously.

Now she was behind her again, the bra held limply in her hand. This time Josephine's hand pulled the bra round to cover her breasts; Emily was pulled forward and the tips of her fingers brushed her nipples. Another growl from behind the curtain.

"So you're from Savannah," said Josephine.

"Yes, ma'am," murmured Emily, clipping up the bra. It burst open and Josephine reached round and attached it with a snap of her fingers.

She turned to Emily, her eyes shining. "Whole lot harder putting it on someone else, huh?" She smiled at her, her front teeth protruding slightly.

"So what's a nice girl like you doing in Paris?" asked Josephine, going over to the make-up table and putting on her lipstick.

"Well, I been playing at some of the jazz halls, uh, they asked me to come in kinda late—"

There was a metallic sound from behind the curtain, a clank of chains; a form leaped up against the material.

"Bananas," said Josephine Baker.

"Huh?"

"Hand me the bananas."

She stood up and stepped out of her shorts and now Emily was alone with the tenderness of her,

40

full and luscious. She was on the point of losing her mind when there was a shriek from outside the door. It was the stage manager.

"Josephine! Now, please, now!"

Josephine snatched the bananas from Emily and, placing one hand on her shoulder for balance, stepped into the panties and pulled them up.

"Thank you."

For a moment she looked straight into Emily's face.

"Young girl in showbiz, huh? Tough getting started. Twelve years ago I was living in a cardboard box in St Louis. Now I'm opening in Paris."

She kissed Emily, gently.

"Go on, they're waiting for you."

"I don't know where—"

"Left, left, left and find a door. Follow it to the orchestra."

The stage manager shouted outside the door. The door squeaked as it started to open. As she was pushing Emily out of the dressing room, Josephine Baker put her lips against her ear and whispered, *"Come back"*.

* * *

Left, left, left led Emily to the pit. The conductor glared at her but the rest of the orchestra moved out of her way. The audience was a murmur behind her as she sat in her seat, took a good long look at the first song sheet and started tuning her violin.

A thin Frenchman was standing nearby, not tuning up but lifting the leg of his trousers and placing a leather guard around his ankles. Emily, still high from her encounter backstage, asked, "What's that for?"

"For the animal," snapped the violinist. With a sigh he pulled up the other leg and slipped a guard underneath the material. When Emily looked around she noticed other musicians doing the same; one cellist wore a body harness beneath his shirt.

"What animal?" asked Emily.

"Chiquita," hissed the violinist.

The lights went out. Her anxiety returning, Emily sank into her seat and picked up her violin.

Chiquita from the dressing room, she thought.

Everything was late tonight, because Josephine Baker's make-up assistant was deep in the embrace of a muscular stagehand, but no one was to know that. Soon the red curtain went up to shouting and applause. The stage was a lush jungle scene, with huge leaves hanging from the ceiling and a fallen tree bisecting the backdrop. Creepers and vines curled along the trunk, while at stage right there was a litter containing a sleeping hunter. Four African porters were sitting on another tree trunk.

Emily was so busy trying to follow the tunes, keeping the rhythm of the orchestra, that she couldn't concentrate on the story playing out on stage; only when the crowd rose to its feet and the young men in the audience howled like wolves did she look up and see a familiar figure creeping down the fallen trunk, splendid in bananas and pearls and the white bra Emily had so recently helped her into.

Josephine Baker ran and slid onto the stage into the splits. She danced a savage dance, her teeth bright, her arms swinging. Her legs were powerful and athletic and she wriggled her belly like a Turkish dancer, all energy and contorting flesh, swaying and turning in a frenzy.

The Parisians were in love with her. How the audience roared as she danced and shimmied, pulling a face and making high-pitched animal noises. Her short black hair was plastered to her forehead, her cheeks inflated comically as she moved her body like a snake.

Emily was enchanted. For the third song she had a moment to sit back and catch her breath, her armpits wet with sweat. Looking around she noticed how many musicians, from the horn section to the strings, had cymbals stacked up next to their chairs. Everyone seemed to be wearing body armour beneath their tuxedos, and Emily felt strangely exposed, like a virgin on an altar.

Josephine marched off the stage at the end of the fourth song. Only when she came walking back holding a length of chain did Emily realise what had been growling behind the curtain. The audience cheered; the orchestra took a step backwards.

Chiquita was a cheetah. She was a very large and very nervous cheetah, her eyes on the clamouring spectators, her diamond collar gleaming. Lost in a frenzy, Josephine danced around her, jumping and falling to the floor like a feline. As the orchestra rose to a trumpet wail Emily saw the tense, worried expressions on the faces of the musicians, like soldiers crouched in a trench awaiting bombardment. She produced a smooth note from her violin and the cheetah turned its golden eyes on her.

Josephine Baker let go of the chain.

The great cat leaped into the orchestra. There was a roar from the crowd. Young men stood and cheered and threw flowers and cigarettes at the stage.

The cheetah hissed at the wind section and was repulsed by trombones; it jumped at the percussionists and scratched at the drummer; the pianist dived into his piano and the conductor hid behind his podium; Chiquita jumped at the string section and was beaten back by a crash of cymbals; for an instant the animal's snarling head was next to Emily's, it's teeth white and razor-sharp. She screamed.

The cheetah was jerked back by the chain. Ms Baker, with effortless strength, dragged it off stage.

The show was over.

The fallen tree was once more behind the red curtain and The Folies Bergères smelled of champagne and cigarettes. Emily was alone in the auditorium, a small woman surrounded by broken bottles and peanuts crushed into the purple carpet.

She was still shaking as she struggled to fit her violin into the case; she was remembering those golden jaws, snapping at her face. At the same time she couldn't forget the dancer's body, her charming smile, the thrill of her skin.

"*Come back,*" whispered the beautiful voice in her mind.

But the next day Emily left Paris.

The Mystery

Josephine Baker (1906-1975) was an American-born erotic dancer, actress and singer. Baker dropped out of school at 12 and lived on the streets of St. Louis, surviving by scavenging for food. Her street-corner dancing attracted attention, however, and she became a professional dancer at age 15.

Success came when she came to Europe and danced at the *Folies Bergères*. Ernest Hemingway pronounced her "the most sensational woman anyone ever saw."

During World War 2 she was highly active within the French Resistance. After the war she was awarded the Croix de Guerre, the Rosette de la Résistance and made a *Chevalier de la Légion d'Honneur*.

Although based in France, she was an active figure in the American Civil Rights movement and was invited, after the assassination of Martin Luther King Jr, to become its leader. She refused the role.

She had a personality as colourful and extraordinary as her live performances suggested *but...*

Did Josephine Baker's cheetah truly attack orchestras in Paris in the 1920s?

Buckingham
Palace Poker

"SHE KNOWS," said Harry.

"Of course she doesn't."

"I've worked at the Palace for over twenty years. There's nothing she doesn't know. She's ubiquitous."

"Just deal the cards, for Christ's sake."

There was the soft sound of cards sliding across the table. All three of us scrutinised our hands in the low light of the lamp.

"Ubiquitous?" said Freddie, grinning. "That's a big word for you, Harry."

"It means everywhere," the old man snapped back.

"She's in Tonga. That's far enough for me."

48

"Yes, I know, but she has spies, she'd fire us for this—"

"Your turn, old man," I said.

Harry slowly put a chip on the table, shaking his head. "She'd fire us for this."

Freddie yawned and stretched, rearranging his tie. He was in his late twenties with brown hair and a mocking voice. I liked his eyes but I didn't like the smile beneath them; there was something sinister there, like a shark in a gentle sea.

"I thought she liked gambling," he said.

"One pound," said Harry, laying out a red chip.

"Two," I said, automatically. Freddie glanced across at me, then back at Harry.

"She likes horse racing, doesn't she?"

"That's sport," said the older man.

"It's still gambling, exactly the same thing. Only the money goes on animals, not cards."

"Horses," grunted Harry, "are not just animals."

"The fact remains."

I watched the passage of a few poker hands, asking myself how Her Majesty would react if she knew about our game. *Unfavourably* was the answer. Fifteen years ago it might have been different; she had a great sense of curiosity and humour when she was younger. These days she seemed reserved when she came to the dog kennels, and I sensed that the old fire was fading.

With a smirk Freddie pushed a pile of chips across the table.

"All in."

"Already?" I was incredulous.

"Keep your voice down," hissed Harry.

"She's in Tonga," said Freddie, "She's on a royal tour, so she probably won't be back for weeks..."

"She *knows*," the older man insisted. "She has a way of knowing things, she knows everything that happens in the palace..."

"Oh really?"

"Yes, really!"

I shushed them, my heart beating hard. Harry was making me nervous. I was remembering a pair of equerries who'd been working for the Duke for years. Just last month they'd got caught spraying each other with hoses; the very next day they'd been replaced. And here I was, playing poker in the palace. *Gambling in the palace.* I wouldn't just get demoted or moved downstairs, I'd get fired, and then what was I going to do? I'd been working for The Family for most of my life, so where would I find a new job at sixty-three?

"She won't even know what poker is," Freddie continued. "She's still living in the 50's."

Harry gave him a wide-eyed, wounded dog look.

"You should have seen her when she got back from Balmoral," said Freddie, stroking his cards. "Wearing that awful orange dress."

"You watch your mouth," snapped Harry.

The betting rose.

"I mean, she's one of the richest women in the world, so why doesn't she employ a stylist to dress her fashionably?"

"That's a matter of opinion."

Freddie shook his head. "Pastel frocks."

"She's a role model to millions, let her wear what she likes."

"You should be careful," I said to Freddie. "Remember that this is a lady who has decades of

51

experience of prime ministers and presidents. She's no one's fool."

They both looked at me in surprise.

"Anyway," smiled Freddie, exposing his shark teeth. He turned to Harry. "All in, old boy."

Harry stared at the chips. He touched his smooth white hair and tugged at his shirt collar. I watched him go through this familiar routine. These tricks were mostly intended for me, as Freddie was too good at poker to be influenced.

"Come on, old boy," said Freddie, softly. He studied Harry with the lazy charm of a cat playing with a mouse.

A smile faltered on Harry's lips and I felt sure he didn't have a good hand. Still he didn't move. He just sat very still, calculating the probabilities, fishing for a response from Freddie. As the evening progressed I was feeling more and more nervous. The sensible part of me wanted to put down my cards and leave the room with my job intact, but the cards on the table were calling to the cards in my hand: I couldn't move.

"Time!" declared Freddie. He produced an egg-timer from under the table.

"Okay, okay…" muttered Harry. He pushed all his chips across the baize and sat looking at them sadly.

I wanted to leave. I wanted to take my money, all fifteen quid of it, swallow my pride and go for the safe option: *sorry lads, enough is enough*. But a small and hungry part of me liked the look of the cards on the table. Now that the stack was high I *had* to see what Freddie and Harry were holding.

"I'll match you," I declared, pushing all my chips across the baize.

There was a moment's silence in the darkened room. No one spoke.

"What's wrong?" I asked. "Too soon?"

There was a scrape of chairs. Both men stood up and stared straight ahead like guilty schoolboys.

"Good Evening, Ma'am," they said.

I turned round, the hairs rising on the back of my neck.

There in the doorway stood The Queen.

I stood and bowed my head.

The Queen came into the tiny office, frowning

behind her glasses. She was wearing a bright orange skirt beneath her overcoat, and I sensed she'd just come in from the cold.

"Cribbage?" she asked, in a faint voice.

"We thought you were in Tonga, ma'am," blustered Harry. "We were taking a small break."

There was a long pause. The Queen scrutinised the table.

"No," she said. "Of course it's not cribbage. You have five cards on the table, and counters. You're gambling."

I held my breath, already running through my job applications for the next day.

"How was your journey—" began Harry.

"There was a hurricane," said the Queen. "And a civil war."

She looked at us over the top of her glasses. We stood examining our fingernails, the floor, the backs of the chairs, anything but the table and the incriminating cards.

"This is my fault, ma'am," Harry began valiantly. "I started this game..."

"One in six," she said quietly.

"Ma'am?"

She was looking down at the table.

"One in six chances...of a Flush."

She came up to my chair and put her hand on the back. She glanced up at me with a smile.

"May I?"

Stunned, moving on autopilot, I pulled the chair back and she gracefully sat down. The three of us stood gawping at her in the dim light. She regaled us with a smile.

"If you wouldn't mind," said The Queen. "Deal me in."

Despite our protests Her Majesty Queen Elizabeth II insisted on shuffling the decks. The cards snapped like rattlesnakes; she dealt quickly and efficiently. Harry and I stared at her, open-mouthed, like fish.

Like any good player she had patience; we watched her hands come down, and an hour had passed before she put down a bet. I lost a lot of money that night; I couldn't concentrate on my own game as I was too busy watching her dexterous fingers, and examining her face for signs of tension or joy when she lifted her cards. For the entire game she wore the same blank expression she gave during her annual speech. She was inscrutable.

Harry did not play aggressively: he would fold whenever she raised the stakes, and that hangdog, guilty look never left his face. But Freddie was merciless; he took to attacking the monarch with glee. Of course he appeared to be deferential and polite, but with each win I saw the faintest flicker of a smirk, like a ripple on a lake. The Queen was not amused, but she never betrayed any frustration.

We weren't playing for high stakes; the buy-in was only fifteen pounds, and big wins rarely topped seventy pounds. What with Harry capitulating every time he was in danger of winning, and my complete inability to concentrate, Freddie began cleaning up on that cool winter's evening.

I remember a big hand coming down at midnight. Harry and I had folded, leaving Freddie facing The Queen in the half-light. Forty pound's worth of chips was piled up at the centre. Soon it was Her Majesty's turn, and she was staring across the table at Freddie through her large reading glasses.

"You could have a seven and a nine," she said slowly. "Although *statistically* I find it highly unlikely..."

She looked down at her cards with a sigh.

"You've been betting very slowly, and I think you're bluffing. But however can I prove that?"

Then, with a nonchalance which horrified me, Freddie reached under the table and produced the eggtimer.

"Time, Your Majesty."

"Frederick, no," hissed Harry.

"Are you bluffing?" The Queen leaned forward in her seat. "I think you may well be."

Freddie just beamed at her, half angel, half shark.

"But I can't tell," she said sadly, and placed her cards on the table, folding a pair of aces.

"Pocket Rockets!" breathed Harry.

For the first time that evening a trace of annoyance passed across Her Majesty's face. I watched the wrinkle deepen and my old fear returned. Was she a bad loser? Would I disappear from the Palace in the morning?

The frown smoothed over like a crease straightened from a sheet. She yawned into her hand, very discreetly. Freddie and Harry and I got to our feet.

"We don't wish to keep Your Majesty up—"

She looked up at us in surprise.

"Whatever's the matter?"

The frown returned.

"We thought it best..." I blustered. "...we thought you might like to retire..."

She raised an eyebrow, surprised. "*Retire?*"

"Oh no, Ma'am," said Harry. "It's just that usually, I mean, we don't play beyond twelve..."

"But I've only just arrived. Unless the three of you are tired..?"

We all sat down and play began again.

I dealt the cards. As we played Harry never lost his worried expression, and I think that each game must have aged him a little more. Freddie grew more and more aggressive towards Her Majesty as the rounds went by. He appeared to be respectful and contrite, but remained as ruthless as ever in his betting. The Queen remained measured and careful.

Gradually, very gradually, things began to change as the dawn approached. Her betting increased and she started making little wins as we grew more and more tired.

Freddie was reluctant to raise her, but he finally succumbed at three thirty. I remember the hand very clearly: there was a pair of twos, with an ace, a jack and a nine on the river. Freddie must have sensed a big win was possible, as he went all in.

The Queen sat straight backed in her chair, her glasses tucked into her grey hair, her posture regal and virtuous.

"Well now," she mused. "You've played this artfully, only going all in on the River, which leads me to believe that you have a high pair…"

As she spoke, her fingers tapped lightly on the table; Freddie didn't respond, just sat very still watching her with the fixed and glittering eyes of a snake.

"…or nothing at all," she said softly.

There was no change in her expression but I knew something had happened. There was a note of triumph in her voice as she declared, "All in" and pushed a hundred pounds worth of chips across the table.

Now I saw something completely new. Freddie's smile remained, but there was something rising in his throat; he was swallowing. An agonising minute passed.

The Queen reached for the egg timer.

Freddie gave a little groan and dropped his cards onto the table. He sat back rubbing his forehead. A beaming Harry pushed Freddie's stack across the baize, and soon Her Majesty was presiding over a red and blue metropolis of poker chips.

Ah, I thought. *There's the old fire.*

With every shuffled deck her winnings increased. As sunlight touched the windowpane the three of us were drooping with fatigue, but The Queen grew stronger and stronger. Soon she reigned supreme at our table, and every time young Freddie swallowed his losses I could have sworn I saw the faintest of smiles on Her Majesty's countenance, like the ripple a shark makes, on a gentle sea.

The Mystery

Elizabeth II was born in 1926 at 17 Bruton Street in London. When her uncle, King Edward VIII, shockingly abdicated the throne after less than a year so as to be free to marry the American divorcee, Wallis Simpson, her father was unexpectedly obliged to become king in 1936 and Elizabeth became heir to the throne.

She succeeded her father in 1952, becoming queen at just 26 years old. She is now the oldest monarch England has ever had and is the reigning queen of sixteen sovereign states including the United Kingdom, Canada, Australia and New Zealand.

She is known to be very keen on horse racing, *but...*

Does the Queen ever play poker with the Buckingham Palace servants?

A Letter
To Stalin

BULGAKOV WAS WOKEN BY THE PHONE. It was a sharp sound, softened by the doors leading from his bed-room to the study. Usually it would make him feel coldly apprehensive, but this afternoon felt different. Perhaps it was the sunlight on his face, so warm for April in Moscow. Or perhaps it was the strange clarity he felt, as he realised his migraine had vanished with the warming of the city.

He sat up in bed, feeling refreshed and hopeful. When he turned to one side the sheets released a smell of perfume, reminding him of the first time he'd met Liubov Evgen'evna as a much younger writer, in 1924. How she'd dazzled him at that party—a vivacious and worldly woman, fluent in

French and well-versed in the literature Bulgakov so loved. That evening he'd forgotten about Count Tolstoy and his party, and he'd laughed in the presence of this magnificent woman.

That was seven years ago. Now he felt a shiver of the same hope, the same yearning. Now he looked up through his bedroom window into the infinite blue. Where he would go if he could fly! Liubov had enchanted him with her stories from abroad, her life in Europe, and Bulgakov had dreamed of France and Italy and Spain; he'd dreamed of freedom, escape from the Soviet Union.

The phone rang on. Now he heard his wife's footsteps on the landing, the miaow of his cat. He wondered who was calling; he had an instinctive fear of the phone, but a knocking at the door was even worse. The OGPU had already searched his apartment and found nothing, but he knew they needed nothing to take him away. That's what had happened to Zemsky: no warning, no crime, just the words of an angry friend in the wrong ear. A knock in the night, a car waiting—vanished.

The slightest hint of criticism of The Party could bring death or exile, but the success of *The Days of the Turbins* had granted Bulgakov an unofficial immunity: the manager at the Moscow Arts Theatre had told him that Stalin himself had seen the play no fewer than fifteen times, and that surely had prolonged Mikhail Bulgakov's life, if not his career.

For his career was in purgatory. Last year in March all of his plays had been banned from public performances; publication of his novels and stories was forbidden, leaving him with the thought, every waking morning: "How will we eat? How will we *eat?*"

That need, that fear, that frustration, had driven him to impulsive acts.

The letters.

How long had it been since the letters?

The ringing stopped. He heard his wife's voice in the study, distant and musical. Bulgakov rubbed his eyes and listened to the distant sound of street cars, the mechanical concert of the city.

The letters.

He may have had a little too much to drink that afternoon, but the emotion he'd poured into those notes had been genuine. He'd written to Gorky, the government, even the Leader himself, describing his persecution at the hands of the press, the vilification of his plays, his slow starvation under the oppression of censorship.

Bulgakov wanted to leave Russia and start a new life. Such thoughts were heresy now: a simple gesture from Stalin could have had him assassinated, but he was starving, so what did he have to lose? He'd heard nothing in reply to the letters: not even a knock at the door.

The writer stretched, fearing the migraine would return, but his mind remained as clear as the sky over Moscow. His bedroom was small and simple. He knew an author of his standing in England or America would enjoy a more luxurious house, and the freedom to go where he wanted; he wouldn't have to write any more allegorical plays in Russia, no more propaganda for his poisoned homeland.

He took a long look around his bedroom. True, he had symbols of prosperity, from the silk gown hanging in the wardrobe, white with a blood-red lining, to the paintings hanging in his hall. On a day like this he could forget his critics. He felt full of a strange hope: one day he would leave here.

On hearing his wife's footsteps outside the door he sat up. He was a svelte man in his late thirties, debonair in a blue suit and red bow tie. His hands were long and elegant, as skilled at creating sell-out plays in the capitol as they'd been treating wounds on the Ukrainian front, over fifteen years ago.

His wife's voice, calling him to the phone. Something in her tone stirred his imagination: who was calling him? Perhaps it was a ship's captain, a pilot or a custom's officer, granting him passage to Europe. It seemed crazy now, but anything could happen on a clear day. He stood up and stretched and took one more look at the open sky and all its possibilities.

Bulgakov walked quickly through the creaking house to his study, where Liubov was waiting with the phone in her hand. She was more corpulent than she'd been at Tolstoy's ball, and her face was worn with worry.

"Who's calling at this hour?" asked her husband.

"From the Central Committee," she said quietly, holding her hand over the receiver.

The writer put his hands on his hips and smiled. His face was angular and handsome.

"What is it, Alexei Afanovich playing his tricks again?"

Then he noticed how pale her face was, her eyes wide and frightened. Still smiling, Bulgakov took the phone.

"Hello?"

A nasal voice came from the receiver.

"Mikhail Afanasyevich Bulgakov?"

"Yes." He winked at his wife.

"Comrade Stalin will talk to you now."

Bulgakov rolled his eyes and turned towards the window. He sighed and stretched, stifling a yawn.

A new voice came on the line.

"I received your letter."

It was soft with a slow Georgian accent millions had heard on the radio. Unmistakable. The blood drained from Bulgakov's face. His body went cold. He leaned to one side, feeling weak. His wife took his hand and he pulled it away from her; he looked at the floor and looked at the ceiling, biting his lip, unable to believe what he was hearing.

"I received your letter," repeated The Great Leader. "In which you expressed your dissatisfaction."

There was no warmth in The Leader's tone. This was no longer the man who'd risen to applaud his play thirteen times. There was doubt in that voice, doubt which could bring Bulgakov a lifetime in Siberia, thirty years' freezing in a Gulag or a knife in the night.

Questions came from the telephone, soft with menace, every word a spring in a trap.

"Do you have any new plays?"

"Yes, I'm continuing to be very productive in my writing."

"Is the theatre treating you well?"

"Yes."

"Are you happy with your work?"

"Yes, I'm overjoyed to be serving the State."

Bulgakov fought to keep his voice steady. Truth was lethal; he had to remain clear-headed and submissive, he had to dig deep for answers, work on automatic, shape every answer to praise the Party, put the Party first; the merest equivocation would put a drop of suspicion into Stalin's mind.

At times the voice on the other side became affable, and the writer felt himself being lulled by it. Yes, the voice was telling him, yes, you can tell me everything, we can talk together as father and son. Bulgakov stared out of his office window, and with every question felt his hopes of a life abroad receding.

"You told me in your letter," continued the voice. "That you wish to emigrate. Do you still want to leave your Motherland, Mikhail Afanasyevich?"

As the words filtered into his ear, Bulgakov felt himself pulled down to earth by a chain; in that voice he felt the dark streets of Russia rising like iron bars around him. A wild part of him wanted to snap the chain, to twist away from Moscow, to freedom. What if he was the first writer to tell Stalin exactly what he thought of his squalid rule; the first man not to bow his head, not to be imprisoned by fear? Why not tell the truth, just once? He took a deep breath.

"I have thought a great deal recently about the question of whether a Russian writer can live outside his homeland," he said slowly.

Tell him, he thought. *Tell him exactly what you feel. Die a brave man.*

He swallowed, closed his eyes.

"And it seems to me he can't."

He bowed his head. His shoulders sagged.

There was a long silence at the other end. For a moment the writer thought The Leader had already disappeared to order his execution.

Stalin coughed. It was a sharp, rattling sound. Bulgakov clung to the telephone, his fingers sweaty, his heart wild in his chest.

"You express yourself well," said The Leader. "I'm sure we can find something useful for you to do. And a place for you to work. Where would you like that to be?"

"In Moscow," Bulgakov heard himself say.

"Good. Perhaps you can write a new play for me. Perhaps we can meet for a longer discussion in the near future. Goodbye, Mikhail Afanasyevich."

The receiver went dead. Bulgakov dropped it on the desk as though it were infected.

"Who was it?" demanded his wife. "What did they say? Tell me."

But the writer was already retreating into himself, sitting at his desk and trying to breathe normally; those fingers which had been so steady performing amputations in his youth were now trembling in his lap. He lit a cigarette and smoked it to the butt; lit another one. A storm was gathering in his mind, the pain returning behind his eyes, stabbing.

The sky was a rich blue over Moscow. Beyond it was Europe and the rest of the world, but now it would have to be imagined. With shaking hands Mikhail Bulgakov pulled the curtain shut, and got to work on a new play.

The Mystery

Mikhail Bulgakov (1891-1940) was a Russian playwright celebrated for the novel *The White Guard* and the play *Days of the Turbins*. Today, Bulgakov is famous for a novel that was not published until 26 years after his death: *The Master and Margarita*, which has been called one of the masterpieces of the 20th century.

Joseph Vissarionovich Stalin (1878-1953) was the first General Secretary of the Communist Party in the Soviet Union. Historians estimate that the total number of citizens killed as a result of Stalin's successive terror campaigns to be around 15 million victims, with around 8 million further deaths due to the famine his agricultural policies caused in the Soviet Union. Stalin died in 1953 from a cerebral hemorrhage he suffered after an all-night dinner.

In 1930, as the first of Stalin's purges were in progress, Mikhail Bulgakov was living and working in Moscow, *but...*

Did Stalin himself telephone Bulgakov as a result of a letter he wrote?

Hemingway's Chihuahua

AS THE DOG CAME INTO THE BAR its head turned from side to side, a pistol with teeth, menacing. Its eyes were tiny and black and it had bone-cracking jaws. It was a beast, an alligator with fur.

The American sailor came in after it, smiling shyly, holding its chain. I pulled my legs up off the floor and tried to protect them with my dress. Two of the local street-dogs exited the bar, their eyes never leaving the brute until they'd run out into the dusty sunlight and down to the quay.

"Well, here she is," said the young sailor, smiling and straining to hold onto the dog.

All eyes in the bar turned to a far corner table. There, splendid in his baggy khaki shorts, his

73

chequered shirt hanging open, sat Papa Hemingway. He was only in his fifties but the big white beard and sunburned skin made him look older. His belly was spread across his hips like a pancake but his arms were thick and muscular.

A smile emerged from under the beard, growing larger as the chain clanked in the sailor's hand. Moving with a slow, nonchalant ease, the big writer leaned down beside his stool and patted a small white head. It belonged to the only animal not to have left the bar: Hemingway's pride and joy, his champion.

"Go get her, boy," came the rich voice from behind the beard.

Hemingway released the chihuahua.

For a man of Hemingway's qualities, from his war record in his twenties to his bullfighting chronicles, his macho novels, womanising and reputation as a magnificent alcoholic, I had been surprised to discover he had such a tiny dog. It didn't seem the right kind of animal for him—a bulldog, perhaps, or an Alsatian, a big dog for a big man, not the rabbit-sized animal I saw him petting in La Terrazza.

I'd followed him to this hot, dim bar all the way from England, where my editor had ordered me to write a piece on the writer's life. My requests to interview Hemingway had been refused. Perhaps he'd smelled a rat when I told him that I had read only one of his novels, and he sensed I was interested more in Hemingway the man than Hemingway the writer. Perhaps it was a distinction he didn't believe in.

So I was refused an interview, but that didn't stop me coming out here to shadow the old boy and enjoy a holiday in the tropical west coast of Cuba. I soon learned that Hemingway divided his time between fishing off the coast of Cojimar, eating extremely well and taking care of his beloved little dog.

Hemingway knew how to hold his liquor, and the reputation of his Papa Dobles was legendary from Havana to Santiago. Now, I could only catch pieces of his conversation in La Terraza, for he spoke such rapid Spanish that I found it difficult to understand, but I guessed that he called the chihuahua Merlin. It took me a while to work out exactly why.

One evening, when Hemingway came in for his drinks and loud, laughing conversation, he placed a bowl of food on the floor and let his dog walk around the bar. No one stroked it. It looked energetic, despite the vicious heat of the afternoon. I sat on my usual bar-stool, feeling like a roasted piece of meat. I'd been trying all day to get the writer to stop and talk to me in Cojimar, but he hadn't responded to me. I knew my editor had given me the job because I was pretty, as well as a fast writer, but it wasn't working so far.

When a group of local fishermen came in, the writer called out to them and they came over to his table. They were small, slow men in peasant jackets and ragged trousers. They watched as a couple of local dogs came in through the doors, and started sniffing round. There was much whispering and soft laughter from the men, and I saw dollar bills being laid on the tabletop, bets.

The intruders were street-dogs, grey and white, scruffy but strong. One of them went straight for Merlin's bowl, but he didn't reach his objective.

The Chihuahua appeared like a white ghost, stopping him. The dog snapped, but it couldn't get close: Merlin started running around him, racing in to bite at his legs, worrying him. At first the street-dog was just annoyed, then he quickly started to look mystified; no matter how fast he turned and snapped he couldn't catch Merlin. Even when both dogs attacked the Chihuahua it danced around them, biting and tormenting them. Finally, snarling and snapping, both dogs were forced out of the bar. Victorious, the Chihuahua waltzed over to its food bowl, its claws clicking on the floor.

I mention this because, over the next couple of weeks, the Terrazza Bar was the only place I was guaranteed to see Ernest Hemingway, and apart from his drinking huge daquiries and telling stories in Spanish, his dog was the only thing I could write about.

For there were many dogs in Cojimar, and all of them seemed to like the Terazza Bar that month. But no matter the size of each new dog, Hemingway's Chihuahua nipped and tormented it into submission; if it didn't roll onto its back with its paws in the air it retreated to the side of the bar, tail between its legs, wide eyed until, accompanied by a shout of laughter from the great writer's table, Merlin chased the confused animal right out of the door.

"You know why they're afraid," said Papa Hemingway in English, and I guessed he was saying it for my benefit, as he glanced across at me with a slow wink. "Why they're all afraid? That's because it's *prodigious*."

"Pro-di-gious?" exclaimed one of the Cuban fishermen, grinning yellow teeth.

"His cock!" boomed the writer. "Everyone's afraid of his prodigious cock!"

Indeed, as the small dog returned to his table there was a vanity in its walk, its pelvis moving from side to side as though he were pulling a heavy weight between his legs. Only Merlin's walk was evidence of anything extraordinary—that and Hemingway's laugh, and the money he made each time a dog was chased squealing from La Terrazza. As if in acknowledgement of its earning power, the Chihuahua walked around the bar with an erect, aristocratic grace which informed everyone, man or beast, who there was the true proprietor of the bar.

Merlin's authority was notorious throughout the region, and it seemed for a while that it would remain unchallenged, until the night the American sailors came into the bar. My baggage was packed and I was preparing to leave Cuba by then; apart from a good sun-tan I'd achieved nothing in Cojimar, learned nothing about Mr Hemingway's life beyond the bar and his boat, Pilar.

I'd tried calling him several times for an interview, but was denied each time. Perhaps he was too busy writing. During the final week I'd sat on the bar stool wearing my shortest dress, trying to make eye contact, and twice approaching him at the bar with a gentle greeting. Each time he said, very gruffly, "I'm not your story."

I'm not your story.

So what was the story? I couldn't make much of his walks down to the harbour, stepping onto his boat and sitting in his fishing chair while his crew took the boat out of the bay. All I had to go on was the size of the fish he caught, and the mocking expression he gave as he passed me on the quayside without a word. I had no idea my piece would finally come to life with the arrival of the sailors on my last night in Cuba.

Their ship must have docked in Havana and they had come down to Cojimar for a little fishing and the hope of a beautiful woman. Some of them were teenagers, boys with flushed faces. When they realised that Hemingway was in the bar they grouped around him in their white uniforms, all speaking at once like excited children.

"Mr Hemingway! Mr Hemingway, sir!"

"I've read all of your novels...."

"Can you sign my book, sir? You didn't write it, but I'd sure love a signature!"

And the great man stood, an expression of affable camaraderie on his face, and I knew he loved the company of fighting men. He looked like a Nordic warrior chief, listening to all the exhortations with a smile.

"You don't read?" he frowned down at one short sailor. "Well, start now."

There was a sudden, frenzied yip. One of the sailors jumped and the writer was on him in a flash, knocking his cap off.

"Damn fool..."

The benign expression had vanished and now he looked like vengeful Poseidon, holding Merlin to his chest and carressing his injured paw. For a moment I was hoping he'd start a fight with the boy and I'd finally have my story, but another sailor, ginger-haired with freckles and a wide innocent face, spoke,

"Gee, Mr Hemingway, is that Merlin?"

"What of it?" snapped the old man.

"Why, I've heard lots of stories, Mr Hemingway, sir. Is it true he can beat any dog that comes in here, sir?"

There was a moment of near silence while the writer petted his Chihuahua, blowing on the injured foot. Finally he set it down and it ran off behind the bar. Hemingway turned on the sailor.

"It's completely true," he said calmly. "What of it?"

"Well, sir, Major Edwards over there said he saw a pretty vicious dog walking about down by the Malecon, and, well, I'd be *curious* to see what would happen if we brought it in here..."

"Well," exhaled Hemingway. He looked round the sailors. Despite their adulatory expressions he must have known they were challenging him, challenging his reputation. I was waiting too. If he agreed I'd have to cancel my flight home.

"Well, well," said Ernest Hemingway, stroking his beard. "That all depends on how much money you'd be prepared to bet."

And so, the next evening, the young officer brought in the alligator dog. He walked up to Hemingway, placed a thick pile of dollar bills on the table, bent down and unchained the monster.

The bitch walked around the room, sniffing every seat. I was guessing she was a cross of Pitbull and Rottweiler, with an extra dose of Doberman thrown in for good measure. Whatever the race, she was demonic. When she came up to my stool I felt a cold horror creep up my legs and I prayed she wouldn't jump at me. She looked straight into my eyes. Yellow foam curled about her muzzle. Her paws were the size of fists.

She turned with a sniff, walked over to a dark corner and urinated. No one, from the barmen to the grizzled fishermen, did anything to stop her; no one, that is, but Hemingway's Chihuahua.

Fearlessly, he came sniffing up, and started jab-
bing away, running round the monster in circles,
nipping and irritating. The beast ignored him. The
Chihuahua paused and stood in front of her, small
and pale with stick legs and a tiny nose, two dashes
of black around his eyes, looking terribly fragile in
front of the black dragon.

There was a moment of complete stillness. The
two dogs stared at each other, weighing each other
up. Then from Hemingway's table there came a low
whistle. The Chihuahua tensed. The black beast
tensed. Another whistle: there was an explosion of
barking and snarling and legs scrabbling, a great
tornado of black and brown and white, chasing
itself round and round the bar. Something thumped
into my stool and I fell shrieking to the floor.

But the dogs weren't interested in me. They were
chasing each other, chasing and biting and barking.
Then I was lifted to my feet and Hemingway's hand
was around my arm, and he was placing his Papa
Doble into my hand to stop the shaking.

The dogs had disappeared. A crowd of young
sailors and ancient fishermen followed the trail of
splintered chairs and broken bottles out of a pas-

sageway at the back of the bar, where a wooden door had been smashed off its hinges.

There was a terrible, high-pitched scream. I realised that Hemingway's dog had finally been caught, and the alligator was tearing him apart. At least it wouldn't last long. We all ran outside the bar, and someone shone a torch at two shapes in the darkness.

"Madre Dios!"

"Holy Cow!"

I hesitated in the doorway. I didn't want to see it. At that moment Mr Hemingway put his hand around my waist and I wanted to fall into his arms; I wanted to hold him and console him on the death of his valiant pet, but when I looked up into his face his strong arms forced me round, forced me to look into the darkness.

The black monster was lying on her front, her great claws stretched out like talons. Blood was gushing from a cut on her head. Perched on her back, like Ahab astride Moby Dick, was Hemingway's Chihuahua. In his mouth a torn chunk of ear, and as he pounded away at his nemesis I realised that the writer's choice of "prodigious cock" was perfect. He thrust for a full minute to the cheers of the drunken crowd; then he paused, climaxed and hopped off.

Merlin bit the beast's rear end and the brute ran away, bleeding and squealing, back through the broken bar and out into the night to the cheers of Cubans and Americans alike.

The Chihuahua danced back into the bar and settled down to eat her ear.

"Well," said Ernest Hemingway, beaming down at me. "There's your story."

The Mystery

Ernest Hemingway (1899-1961) was an American novelist whose simple style of writing greatly influenced 20th century fiction. He was awarded the Nobel Prize for Literature in 1954 but was also equally celebrated for his travels and adventurous lifestyle, which frequently formed the basis of his novels. *A Farewell to Arms,* for example, was based on his experiences as an ambulance driver in the First World War, *For Whom The Bell Tolls* was inspired by his time as a reporter covering the Spanish Civil War, and *The Old Man and the Sea* was inspired by his love of deep-sea fishing. Hemingway loved blood sports such as bullfighting, and maintained residences in Florida and Cuba during the 1940s, *but...*

Did Ernest Hemingway have a lethal Chihuahua in Cuba?

Death
in Hollywood

THAT MUST HAVE BEEN AN HOUR, maybe two hours
before the man in the blood covered suit came in.
I say blood drenched but it only covered his shirt.
Valerie reckoned he was Errol Flynn but who could
tell.

The station was quiet for a Saturday night
shift; quiet enough to follow a fly from fan to fan.
Three drunks had been pulled in and locked up
and I had nothing to do but watch Dwight trying
to charm Valerie. He was perched on the edge of
her desk, rolling a pencil between his fingers while
the secretary sat as uninterested as ever, using her
typewriter as a barricade. I couldn't hear them
through the glass, but since I was sitting at the

back of a dark office they couldn't see me either. It was fun.

Deputy Dwight was going nowhere. As he rocked back and forth, telling silent jokes, I watched Valerie's tiny red mouth for signs of life, but she remained calm and composed.

She was a little too pretty for a desk job but not pretty enough for much else. Her brown hair was tied back in a bun and her glasses worked well with her round face. There was a touch of mischief in her smile but only a touch. I liked the arch of her eyebrows and her habits of ribbons and bows, and she carried herself well, straight backed with a lazy lilt when she was standing up or sitting down. There was a lot of promise in those brown eyes.

Dwight stood up nonchalantly, two hundred pounds of cop, one ounce of brain. He looked disappointed; I wondered what he was saying to her.

"Excuse me, sir."

Another of my deputies, Clarkson or Reeves, was standing in the doorway. Beside him stood a tall man with his hat in his hands. Handsome and a little arrogant, I thought, and his dinner jacket needed a wash for all that blood.

"Yeah," I said.

The tall man came forward and held out his hand.

"Well, I'm sorry to disturb you...my friend has had an accident."

"Nearby?"

"Yes..." He ran his hand through his oily hair. "Yes, I need a doctor, right now. Can you do that for me?"

There was some Irish in that voice mixed with something else. He was drunk but controlling himself, hiding it behind the soft tones of a movie star. A lot of them lived round here. I didn't have much time for them rich people. I felt my jacket for my cigarette case and looked through the big glass window.

They'd noticed the new arrival. Dwight was standing, wide-eyed and stupefied, by the desk, and Valerie was getting to her feet like a cat waking in a pool of sunshine. A flush was coming to her cheeks.

"Sir?" said the tall man. "You need to come out straight away." His hands were shaking and a look of horror crossed his face. Even so, when the door opened and Valerie entered the room, he straightened up a little. There was a quick smile, and he patted his hair out of habit.

"Miss."

There was a honeyed silence. Valerie stood in the doorway, transfixed.

Dwight's low voice broke the spell. "Damn, that's Errol Flynn."

I looked at him. "Huh?"

"I saw you in *Captain Blood*," said Dwight. "And *Robin Hood*. Man, you sure showed them with that sword!"

"You must have me confused with someone else," the man said quickly. "It happens quite often—"

"Errol Flynn," breathed Valerie Vandelier. Her tongue darted out and dabbed her lips. She looked like she wanted to eat him.

"Dwight," I said curtly. "The gentleman says there's been an accident, so you and I will accompany him to the scene. Officer Clarkson—"

"Reeves, sir."

I put a hand to my temple. "Reeves, yeah. You and the other guy stay here."

"Please," said the bloodstained man. "We need to hurry." He turned to leave and Valerie started to follow him. She was sleepwalking.

"You stay here," I said. I left before she could raise those deep Spanish eyes at me.

* * *

Outside it was quiet. Quiet enough to hear the sea in Santa Monica, quiet enough to catch the scratch of a needle sleeping on a gramophone. The air was hot and thick enough to drown in. It was humid and fragrant and you could almost smell the jazz coming up from the cellar bars. The good-looking guy who, as far as I was concerned, wasn't Errol Flynn, led us down Ocean where the breeze should have been. He didn't seem nervous.

We went up Bay Street, an avenue of palms which pointed into the sky. Coconut husks littered the sidewalk. The bushes on either side were thick and fat. We passed a light in a dark house, watching like an eye, and I was finding it hard to keep up with the bloodstained man; Dwight was ahead of me, but I was near enough to see the gentleman stop at a tree, bend down and give a little sob. Then he backed away, his eyes wide and fearful.

"Dwight!" I yelled. But the big deputy was resting against the trunk, his back turned to the creamy figure at his feet, fumbling for a handkerchief and vomiting up through his fingers.

"Dwight!" I shouted. "Handcuff him!"

"Just a minute, Sarge…"

He bent double and vomited in front of me. He straightened up panting, his face pale with revulsion.

"Cuff him!" I said. To my surprise the blood-stained man didn't run, he just stood and exhaled wearily into the night as my deputy pulled his hands behind his back. Dwight took him to one side, leaving me with his handkerchief, the bushes lining the sidewalk and the naked girl.

Well, she was almost naked. Her panties had made it to her ankle but that was as far as they went. If I'd thought her boyfriend had blood issues, this was a whole different league. The girl was resting against the palm tree. Her hands were clenched but the rest of her was completely relaxed, newly dead.

There was an expression of surprise on her face and her head was broken.

I stood back, my heart beating hard. I'd seen dead people before, but no one hit as hard as this. This was beyond an axe, or a hammer. This was complete destruction, from the piece of skull on the palm tree to the blood and brain glistening on her shoulderblade. I couldn't believe a man could be so strong and so angry as to strike a girl like this, a beautiful young girl with moonlit skin and mystified eyes. I took off my jacket and laid it across her.

"Shucked," came a voice behind me.

Instinctively I stepped across the body of the girl.

"I told you to stay inside!"

Valerie stepped out from behind a high bush. She was barefoot and that explained how I hadn't heard her.

"Stay back!" I warned her. "It's murder. Ain't for you to see."

But she brushed past me like a cat, curious.

"Shucked," she murmured, looking down at the girl.

"What?"

"Shucked like a husk of corn. Ain't murder."

She looked up at the top of the tree, then back at me, her face shining with moonlight.

"No one killed no one," she said.

"We're charging him with the murder of a woman…"

"He was out of control."

"You bet your ass he was out of control. Now get back to the station."

Still looking up, she paced round the tree, moving with a deliberate, waltzing lilt.

"…he just couldn't wait, could he?"

She glanced across at the handsome man. There was understanding in her eyes; he stared back at her with an intense, fixed expression, like a drowning man seeing an island.

"It must have been hard," she mused, stroking her chin with a red nail. "Hard, fast and violent. He just couldn't wait, and once he'd started…"

It seemed to me she knew something; or at least, suspected it.

"They both couldn't wait…" she murmured "…so he unzipped her…unpeeled her…"

She paused, searching for the right word.

"Like a banana."

Revolted, I felt my hand snake around her hip. She pulled away and slapped the tree. "Right here, both of them, he probably lifted her up—"

"And killed her," I repeated, adamant. The tall man looked away.

Valerie shook her head, her eyes full of disdain. Then she got on her hands and knees and crawled away into the bushes. I realised I was breathing hard. I looked across at the bloodstained gentleman and saw an expression of hope beginning to cross his face, as though he were remembering something.

As for me, I had to go back to the station and file the report that Valerie was meant to be typing up, and not hiding in the bushes.

"Miss Vandelier, what the hell—"

"Aha!" She shot to her feet, exultant. She looked up to the top of the tree, then held her arm out to me, shyly.

In her hand was a bloody coconut.

The Mystery

Errol Flynn (1909-1959) was an Australian-born actor and one of the biggest movie stars during Hollywood's golden years, the leading man of numerous action movies such as *Captain Blood* and *Robin Hood*.

He was celebrated also for his flamboyant, partying lifestyle and innumerable sexual conquests. In 1942, his lifestyle got him in serious trouble when two under-age girls accused him of having raped them. The subsequent court case was a national sensation, but Flynn was cleared of the charges and his reputation as a lothario only increased.

There are numerous tales of his sexual conquests and scandalous lifestyle, *but...*

Did Errol Flynn accidentally cause the death of a woman in 1942?

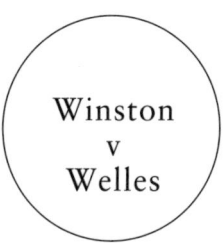

Winston
v
Welles

"CUT!"

Orson Welles, corpulent in the midday sun, clasped his hands behind his head and breathed deeply. His dark facepaint was running down his collar. There was a stench of Italian sewage on the air, which for Welles added to the movie; somehow it *smelled* Shakespearean. It was the kind of paradox he'd normally enjoy, but today he was facing a problem. A large, scowling problem.

Welles cleared his throat and cupped his hands over his mouth.

"Mr Churchill ...perhaps you should..."

His voice ran off like water down a drain.

Damnit, I never should have agreed to this.
True, the ex-Prime Minister had bowed to him in the Venetian café, inspiring a Russian financier to help save *Othello*, but now he was threatening to crash the movie.

Orson Welles was shooting a meeting of senators in Rome. The cathedral was huge and full of the kind of shadows much loved by the director. It should have been a simple take, but how can you replicate Shakespearean when the single most recognizable man in modern times was on set? Sir Winston wasn't even smoking a cigar, just standing beside a stone pillar.

Orson sat in his foldaway chair, brooding. There beneath the arch, dressed in a fur jacket and cap, the great leader brooded back at him. The fierce eyes were set deep in the folds of his face, and he seemed proud and immovable. Mr Welles was well aware of the man's pride at stake; only last year he'd been voted out of office after leading his country to the greatest victory in modern times.

Winston Churchill, with a slight bow in a cafe, had earned Mr Welles the financing he needed to shoot *Othello*. Welles had suggested the role of an extra as a joke to the great Englishman, and was surprised when he'd agreed to do it. He'd underestimated Churchill's wicked sense of humour, not to mention his ambition. The American had felt it was amusing at the time, but now, on the thirtieth take, he had no recourse but to ask Mr Churchill to step down from the set.

The great man's body language was all wrong, and it was painfully obvious he wasn't an actor. He'd never blend in, no matter how many changes of wardrobe Welles gave him. It didn't work, but what could the director tell him now? How could he remove him without causing a scandal, destroying the *Othello* shoot and humiliating both of them?

Orson Welles swallowed, cleared his throat and cupped his hands to his lips.

The Mystery

Orson Welles (1915-1985) is celebrated as one of the most influential film directors of all time. His first film, *Citizen Kane,* which he also wrote and played the lead role in, is consistently voted the greatest film of all time by critics. His relations with the Hollywood studios were very strained, however, and throughout his subsequent career he had constant difficulty raising the finance for his films.

Winston Churchill (1874-1965) was a British politician and prime minister of the nation during the Second World War, when his firm leadership and oratorical skills played a central role in maintaining Britain's morale during the darkest periods of the conflict. A prolific writer, principally of works of history, he was awarded the Nobel Prize for Literature in 1953, *but...*

Did Orson Welles hire Winston Churchill as an extra in 1949?

Follow
the
Song

"ABO. YOU, BOY."

Amaroo looks up. He has to look up.

"You hearing me, you speak English? Nod if you understand me, Abo. Just nod, there's the boy."

The Aborigine nods his head. The man clears his throat and spits saliva onto the orange dust. He points a thumb at a tall thin man, another White-fella.

"Jerry here tells me you walked here from the Western Territories. Walked all the way, that right?"

Amaroo looks at him. The speaker is short with years of muscle on his arms, big arms. Maybe forty. His face is lined and heavy and all the laughter is gone a long time ago. No love on his face. His years are bitter. He's wearing blue and grey overalls and a grey shirt like all the other workers on the site.

"Leave him alone, Mick," says the taller man. "Maybe he can't speak."

But Mick is more persistent. "Answer me boy!"

Amaroo nods and he gives a big empty laugh and claps his friend on the back. Jerry is much younger than him but they have the same smile.

"Listen to him!" laughs Mick. "From Kalgoorlie Boulder! That must be all of fifteen hundred miles!"

"Says he sang all the way," says Jerry. They grin at each other, but when the Aborigine smiles they stop smiling.

"Why you lying, boy?" asks the short man. He comes up close. "Why?" His voice is softer now. He pushes Amaroo's shoulder.

"You hear that Jerry? These Boongs are always making up these stupid stories. Walking without maps."

Behind them comes a metallic clanking noise. A platform is being constructed by some of the supervisors. Beyond that is scaffolding and the skeleton of Sydney Opera House; beyond that, sunlight glitters on the harbour.

Jerry scratches the sunburn on his neck, looks at the platform, touches his friend's shoulder.

"Danny at the outstation says they get Abos coming clear across the bush without a stitch on them. Says they know the way, they don't need maps."

Mick spits again in the dust.

"Something to do with the singing," Jerry goes on. "Like, they have a song for every journey. Songs for every rock and bush and hill they see…"

Mick laughs straight in Amaroo's face, so close he spits in his mouth. The Aborigine doesn't react, doesn't grimace at the man's sour breath. He bends his head, keeping himself lower than the White-fella, so careful to look submissive that he looks like a beaten animal. His arms are like hard dark ropes and his face is wide and the sweat in his hair glistens in the winter sun.

There is more clanking from the platform, then the shriek of feedback from a microphone. Now there are big speakers being put up, with a silver microphone stand at the centre. Important looking people in hats are gathering around, discussing something.

"What's all this, Jerry?" asks Mick.

"Heard there's some movie star come to talk to us. Come all the way from America."

"I expect he sang his way here." Both men break up laughing.

"New York, New York," intones Mick, and Amaroo looks away. There's no learning in his voice.

Jerry leans on his shovel and wipes the sweat from his hair with a rag.

"Danny says he's a Communist and the Yanks took his passport away."

"A Commie! What's a Commie doing in Australia?"

"Don't ask me, mate."

Both men seem so preoccupied with each other that Amaroo tries to move away, slowly and quietly, but Mick catches him by the neck and pulls him back.

"You ain't finished telling us about your journey. You with the songs, you blackies with your songs in the bush. Now, if that's a fact, what's the song for this shovel here, eh? You must have a song for that, eh?" He shakes the Aboriginal's collar, so hard that Amaroo loses his balance and falls in the dust. Amaroo is breathing hard, face down. His vision blurs with tears of rage.

"What's the song for that, eh?" Mick slaps him. "Go on, sing us a song, boy. Tell us where you've been. Sing me a map. Sing me to Canberra, that's the boy, eh?" Jerry is helpless with laughter. Now there are other men gathering round, mostly white construction workers, but many of them are moving off towards the platform. Amaroo tries getting to his feet and Mick gives him another shake and he falls to the dust like a pile of sticks.

"What's the matter, Mick?" says one voice.

"Abo giving you problems?"

"...leave the poor bugger alone..."

"...give him a kick..."

There's more harsh feedback from the microphone.

"Um, gentlemen…" It's the foreman's voice, upper-class and apologetic. "Gentlemen, it's my great pleasure, ah…great pleasure to welcome a very special gentleman to the site. Fresh from the United States."

"Commie," says Mick. He releases Amaroo and turns to the platform. From between the workmen's shoulders he sees the crowd on the platform part, and a tall figure in a suit and beret comes up to the microphone.

"Of all things!" exclaims Jerry. "Not another Boongie!"

Something sinks inside Amaroo. The American's a Blackfella, he thinks, brought here for the entertainment of all these Whitefellas.

The announcer continues speaking, and Amaroo hears a lot of words he doesn't recognise, including a completely new word, "Robeson". Now, as the man in the suit steps up to the microphone, Amaroo wonders why he left his people, just so he could be standing alone and exposed to these unloved men. *Just like me*, he thought.

I could've stayed in the red land, but for what?
For the drunk, the beer? Where am I now? I have
no direction here.

The man on the stage clears his throat. The crowd murmur to themselves, craning their necks to see better.

A voice comes among them.

It's low and warm; it flows like a deep river, like early sunlight, like midnight fire. It reaches under Amaroo, it lifts him up. The song ends and another begins. The workmen are held by it, and by the next three songs, and it's deeper than any sound they've ever heard. Mick glances at Amaroo but now he is taller than Mick, he looks down on him because he is strong with that voice now.

For a terrible moment Robeson stops singing, but now he is coming down off the platform and walking among the tired workers, he is talking and laughing with the men among the bones of the opera house, and Amaroo pushes past Mick and comes closer, and there is the singer, there is that great man, this king with the body of a bear, beaming with bright happy teeth and talking among the men.

And there, just ten feet away, he sings. Amaroo is raised like a ship on a strong wind. He is a child hearing his father again. He closes his eyes and opens his body to the song. The voice takes him away, it takes him across faraway seas, it takes him past cities and waterfalls; it brings him the pain of his people, the torment and despair, the hopes and the failures, the hatred and the fire, the deliverance from servitude. It brings Amaroo his name, and he whispers it to the red earth:

"Beautiful land."

And Amaroo sees Jerry standing like a lost child, and Jerry is weeping through his fingers. The deep river words touch him and touch every man on the site, and rich in his voice is the power of forgiveness. Paul Robeson sings about America; he sings the land into existence. Amaroo follows the song.

The Mystery

Paul Leroy Robeson (1898-1976) was the son of an escaped slave, and became famous the world over as a bass-tenor singer, in particular thanks to the song *Old Man River*.

He was an early voice in the Civil Rights movement, and is cited by numerous African-Americans as the first man to embody pride in his African heritage and dignity as a black actor.

His political views and frequent criticism of America's treatment of blacks were to cost him dear: in 1950, at the height of his fame and success, his passport was confiscated. Confined to the USA, he was subject to a campaign of censorship: his songs were no longer played on the radio, his films were not shown in the cinema and it was increasingly difficult to buy his records.

After an international campaign and a Supreme Court ruling, his passport was restored in 1958 and he once again began to tour the world but...

Did Paul Robeson sing to the men constructing the Sydney Opera House in 1960?

If you enjoyed this book, don't miss the
other titles from the **paper planes** collection.

Here is an excerpt from:

Sorceress

Philippa Boston

Chapter 1

THE CLEAR AUGUST SKY over Oxford was darkening rapidly as Maude Mansfield hurried across the quadrangle of Christ Church College. Although she was not a timid girl, the first thunder-clap of the storm made her jump as she emerged from the college onto the crowded city street.

To her left the South Gate was busier than usual. People outside the city walls had seen the storm approaching across the fields and were moving fast to take refuge. Carts, animals and people pushed and jostled to get through the gate.

Maude had not realised there was a storm coming. The day had been hot and humid, as had every day for weeks now. Some of the older people said 1583 was the hottest Summer since a Queen sat on the throne. It was an intense heat that turned the milk and made the meat go bad. The towns-people sweated, the sewage and the rubbish in the gutters rotted, and the city stank.

By the time Maude reached Brewer Street the first fat drops of rain began to fall. She pulled her cloak further over her head and around her body, feeling irritated with her elder sister.

"Jane has another tummy ache! For the love of God! I am glad not to be such a feeble example of womanhood! And yet I have to play her servant girl." She hurried on her way towards the house of the woman who sold healing potions.

The rain now started to fall in thundering sheets. The damp smell of fermentation from the brewery filled Maude's nostrils as she ran towards the corner.

Although not being a 'feeble example of womanhood' like her sister, Maude yelped with shock as even louder lightning ripped across the sky, and she thumped straight into a similarly-hooded figure rushing the other way. They both cried out in surprise.

"My apologies!" shouted Maude, over the noise of the storm.

"No mine, indeed, ma'am!"

"Susan?" Maude said, seeing it was the potion seller.

"Mistress Mansfield? 'Tis you! Why in God's name are you out in this storm?"

"Why I am going to your house, Susan, for a potion for Jane!" Maude said, pulling Susan O'Flaherty out of the rain to shelter under an ornate doorway. "And surely I could ask you the same question? Why are *you* out in this?"

"Oh Mistress Mansfield, I cannot stop! A lady staying at the Flying Horse Inn has called for me—she's taken terrible sick and needs my help, the messenger said. But I am supposed to keep complete secrecy, Mistress Mansfield, oh Lord!" Susan put her hand to her mouth, "I was to tell no one and here I am telling you! You must just forget—I never said nothing, d'you see? Why she wants me, I don't know. It's apothecaries who usually get called to smart taverns like the Flying Horse, not people like me."

"But you are the best potion-maker in the whole of Oxford, Susan!" Maude protested, "That's why I was on my way to see you— to get an infusion for Jane. It's her tummy— again! I will walk with you and take your advice, if I may."

The two women hurried back along Brewer Street towards the centre of the city, bent against the driving rain.

"Tell her to drink an infusion of the chamomile I gave you for now," Susan O'Flaherty said as they walked, "If you come to my house tomorrow morning I'll give you some other herbs that will help. And remember— place warm stones on the muscles. Now I must go on, if you will excuse me, Mistress. The man was most insistent I hurry. God bless you and keep you dry, Mistress."

"God bless you too, Susan! 'Til tomorrow then, in the morning."

Chapter 2

"WHAT DO YOU MEAN 'SHE'S GONE,' PATRICK?" asked Maude, looking down at Susan O'Flaherty's little boy the next morning. "She told me especially to come at this time."

"She said she might be gone an hour or two, Mistress Mansfield," said the young boy, frowning against the bright morning sun, "but she has been out all night and not sent word to us."

"But that's not like her, Patrick. Not a word, nothing?"

"Nothing, Mistress," the boy confirmed unhappily, "I went to the Flying Horse Inn to ask after her and they sent me away most nastily. They called mother a sorceress and said they wouldn't allow the likes of her past the door. And they hit me, Mistress, hit me so hard my ear is still hurting from the blow."

"The monsters!" said Maude, rubbing the poor boy's ear. "I know she was there. She was specially asked for— she told me."

"It's true, Mistress, we all heard the man ask for her —urgent like— didn't we?"

The other two, even smaller children nodded vigorously at Maude, their neat little brows furrowed with concern.

"'Flying Horse Inn' he said, clear as day. And then the storm, and she ain't come back…"

Tears welled up in the eyes of the brave little boy, fists clenched at his sides as he struggled to keep control of his fears.

Maude hugged him to her and the other two instantly fell upon her skirts too. She glanced desperately around the room as the three children cried, hoping to see some explanation. But there was nothing to help her except silent bottles of herbs and potions.

Chapter 3

"SUSAN O'FLAHERTY is locked in Bocardo, Maude."
Harry informed her the next morning, he and his
friend John de Courcy having made enquiries about
town.

"Bocardo?" Maude frowned, "But why? No
one is locked in Bocardo anymore unless they must
be quarantined?"

"She is accused of witchcraft, so they say." he
explained, "And is confined in Bocardo away from
other souls so she does not acquaint them with
Satan's ways. They say she shouts about the plague
and has the sweating sickness."

"But who accuses her?" Maude asked in horror.

"The Reverend Stoneworthy, who preaches out of St Clement's Church."

"That humourless fellow that shouts about sin in the Corn Market?"

"The same," Harry confirmed. "He is her main accuser, and he has witnesses, of course: townspeople suspicious of poor Susan. A witch trial always brings out the venom in people."

"I knew it! Didn't I say, Harry?"

"You did."

"And I was right!"

"You were."

Maude was so fired up with excitement and indignation that she was unaware of the effect she was having on the young man. As she walked to and fro in her well-cut morning gown, her chaotic curls falling down her back and the flush in her cheek, Harry quite forgot why he was there.

"We must talk to her, Harry."

"To who?"

"To *Susan*, you goose. Who did you think: Queen Bess?"

"We cannot. She is locked up all alone and none may go near her. They say her witchery has made her mad."

"What tosh! She has caught a chill in the storm, that is all, as any woman would who gives all her food to her children and then gets cold and wet. I'd bet my life on it. I will find a way to see her Harry."

"But what if it is the pestilence?"

"You may stay with the guard creating a distraction. I will see the situation with Susan."

"But what of the Flying Horse?"

"Of course— I have not told you! The tavern keeper is willing to swear on the great Bible that there was no one sick in the tavern that night."

"He said that?"

"To me, yesterday. Nobody with any sickness at the tavern since last Spring's ague. No knowledge of Susan being there either. I could not speak long with him as he was heading off on his cart and was in a hurry. But he said he would swear on the great bible."

"Which is worth nothing if he is a closet papist," added Harry cynically.

"He did not seem the type."

"What is he like, this tavern keeper?"

"He is a charming man, most polite. He was very apologetic that he did not have the time to climb down to speak at that time, and invited me, with such a very friendly smile, to return to take a mug of something and talk more if I wished. And he is an Associate of the Mayor too — at such a young age…"

Harry noticed that Maude was blushing slightly and fixed her with a hard stare.

"What do you mean 'young age'?"

"Well he can't be more than thirty years of age…"

"That *old*?"

"It's not *that* old."

The door opened and Jane Mansfield entered, halted when she saw Harry in the room and instinctively raised a hand to check her hair. She smiled up at him through her eyelashes.

"Why Sir Harry, you are come so early to visit?" She smiled her most winning smile at the handsome legal scholar.

"Good morning, Miss Mansfield," said Harry with a bow. "Yes, I have come to inform your sister of the whereabouts of the apothecary…"

"You have found her finally? There, Maude— didn't I tell you she would turn up?" Jane smiled triumphantly at her sister.

"Not exactly turned up, Miss Mansfield. My friend John de Courcy made enquiries on her behalf and discovered she is held in Bocardo."

"Mr de Courcy?" gasped Jane, indifferent to the news that Mrs O'Flaherty was in gaol. "Why would such an important man as Mr de Courcy be making enquiries about that woman?"

"Because she helped prove his innocence —you might remember, sister— when we all believed him innocent and the rest of the world did not? Do you remember sister? And 'that woman', as you call her, testified on his behalf, even at great personal risk to herself and her children?"

Jane blushed at the memory of her own lack of belief in John de Courcy's innocence and her willingness to listen to the venomous lies of his enemies.

"Of course, I remember. It is kind of him to give his time to the woman, even so."

"I suppose my friend John feels that he must repay the favour because he is that sort of a man, Miss Mansfield: full of integrity."

Jane frowned slightly, unsure whether Harry too was making fun of her or not.

* * *

Maude, clothed in her dark cloak, too hot for the end of summer, but necessary to preserve her identity, emerged from the door that led from the back of the Master's lodgings onto the lane between the south side of the college and the Meadow beyond.

She made her way up South Street and battled through the carts and people fighting their way through the main crossing point of the city, known as the carre-forks, and on down the Corn Market towards the North Gate.

She spotted Harry and John waiting as planned, by the New Inn.

As she approached, Harry was telling John about their teasing of Jane.

"Poor Jane!" said Maude. "She looked as though she had swallowed an artichoke! We must stop persecuting her on Mr de Courcy's behalf, Sir Harry."

"Indeed you must!" said John, a little too vehemently. Maude and Harry turned curious expressions on him.

"*Must* we, Mr de Courcy? And why might that be? I thought that now you were courted by so many smart maids of Oxford, you no longer thought of my sister?"

"Miss Mansfield, I am *not* courted, indeed I am *not*, by anyone —who are these maids you speak of? And your sister— well, of course I think —I mean...why, I don't know what— well, I just don't believe in making fun of people..."

Maude and Harry laughed at John's stammering embarrassment. Harry clapped a hand on his friend's shoulder.

"Now don't you worry, Johnny, we are only ribbing you too. You think about whatever or whomever you want to think about. Now— to the job in hand."

"Are you decided on your part, Mr de Courcy?" asked Maude.

John nodded and pointed toward a man further along the street from them, waiting with a basket of bread.

"Good luck! I'll be as quick as I can. Sir Harry— lead on to hell on earth!"

The guard moved eagerly towards the window to look down upon the North Gate, always a lively spot. Below, a young gentleman scholar seemed to have collided with a baker carrying a tray. Loaves of bread were rolling around in the street and an argument was in progress. As they watched, a dark-cloaked figure moved swiftly across the room towards the cells.

ABOUT THE AUTHOR

Over the last fourteen years, Peter Flynn has
worked in schools, prisons and zoos in China,
Madagascar and Peru. His writing has previously
been published in *Tank*, and his travel pieces
have been broadcast on BBC Radio 4.
His 2006 play *The Girls* was a massive success
at London's Courtyard Theatre.
Hemingway's Chihuahua and Other Mysteries
is his first work of prose fiction.

Hemingway's Chihuahua
on www.paperplanes.fr:
- the audio version read by Saul Jephcott
and Karin Morgan
- Peter Flynn talks about writing
Hemingway's Chihuahua